SECRET
of
the STONES

TONY BRADMAN

With illustrations by
Martin Remphry

Barrington Stoke

For my cousin Trevor Bradman –
gone, but not forgotten

First published in 2017 in Great Britain by
Barrington Stoke Ltd
18 Walker Street, Edinburgh, EH3 7LP

www.barringtonstoke.co.uk

Text © 2017 Tony Bradman
Illustrations © 2017 Martin Remphry

A CIP catalogue record for this book is available
from the British Library upon request

ISBN: 978-1-78112-754-4

Printed in China by Leo

Contents

Chapter 1
A Storm Coming

My name is Maglos. My father is the High Chief of my tribe, the Guardians of the Great Temple. His name is Daguno and I am his only son. Listen now as I tell you the story of how I was cast out of the light and into the darkness. How I was lost, and how I found my way again.

Listen closely. For this is the story of how I died, and came back to life ...

*

My story begins on a summer morning. I woke up early to go fishing in the river near our village, but my father stopped me as I was leaving the great hall. We stood side by side in front of its doors and looked over the huts at the wide plain beyond. In the distance we could see the Great Temple, its giant stones grey in the soft light of dawn. Thick clouds were moving in from the west, and I knew they would bring a rain storm.

"Stay with me today, Maglos," my father said. "I have a feeling I will need you."

He was frowning, and seemed troubled, but that wasn't unusual. I knew it wasn't easy to be High Chief. The Great Temple was a holy place, the gateway between the Land of the Living and the Land of the Dead. People came from near and far to have their new babies blessed here, and to bury their dead chiefs. They came to the festivals of the sun in summer and winter. They came to make sacrifices to the Gods.

And so, my father, as the High Chief, was always busy. He had to make sure things were

done in the right way, especially the prayers and the rituals – the High Chief was a priest as well as a leader. The people who came needed shelter, they needed food and they needed to be cared for. And people can be difficult, so there were often problems to be sorted out. But in the last few days, my father had been more worried than normal, and I guessed why.

"Of course I will stay with you," I said. "But what is wrong? Has Tigran done something?"

"Not yet, my son – it is what he might do that makes me feel uneasy."

"Why is he always so horrible to you?" I asked. "He is your brother. Why aren't you friends?"

"There is great love in families," my father said, "but there can be great hate too." He gave a sigh. "I only hope that one day Tigran will see we can be friends again ..."

4

'Such a thing will never happen,' I thought, but I said nothing. Tigran was my father's younger brother, and once they had loved each other and played together. They had always looked alike – both were strong, their backs and arms broad, their hair black like that of most of the tribe. People said I looked just like them too.

But my father and uncle had grown up to be very different from each other – as different as two brothers could be. My father was kind and thoughtful. Tigran had become a warrior – he loved to fight and, sometimes, to be cruel. He often said my father was weak, and that he, Tigran, should be High Chief.

I hated Tigran for the way he treated my father. My mother had died of a winter sickness when I was still a baby, 12 summers before, and my father had not taken another wife. My father and I were very close, and I knew just how brave and wise a man he was.

Only one person could be High Chief after him, and that was me. In our tribe, when the High Chief dies, it is his oldest son that takes his place.

"Will Tigran come back from his hunting trip today?" I said.

"Yes," my father said. "He sent one of his men ahead of him to tell us he would be back before sundown."

"I wish he would go hunting more often," I said. "Things are better when he and his band of warriors are away."

My father smiled. "Perhaps he will surprise us this time, and be kind," he said.

Then he looked up at the sky. "I sense a storm ... Come, let us see to the people who arrived yesterday, and make sure they have everything they need."

Tigran and the rain storm both arrived later that day, one after the other. The rain fell, a gusting wind blew it sideways. Lightning flickered and crackled over the plain, and the Gods spoke in the dark sky. The deep thunder of their voices rumbled above our heads.

Tigran returned just as the storm finished. He ran in the village gate with his men, their tunics wet from the rain, their legs thick with mud. Two of the men carried the body of a fine deer, slung on a wooden pole between them.

"Greetings, brother," my father said. "I see you have had good hunting."

Then Tigran did surprise us. I expected him to show off to his warriors by saying something sharp or mean to my father, the way he always did. He stopped, as if he wanted to speak, but then he seemed to change his mind. He frowned instead and turned away to go to his own house.

As I watched Tigran go, I felt a chill run down my spine.

Chapter 2
Blood on the Altar

Tigran stayed quiet, and he kept out of our way too. We hardly saw him for the next few days, and soon I forgot my worries about him. My father and I were very busy – we were close to the day of the mid-summer festival.

Nobody could remember who built the Great Temple long, long ago. My father said the Gods themselves must have helped. Who except the Gods could have moved such huge stones to stand them in two rings, the smaller one inside the larger? The stones stood in such a way that two times a year – in mid-summer and mid-winter – the rising sun would shine a beam on the Sacred Altar at the heart of the inner ring. As long as the right sacrifice was made.

Many people come to see such a wonder. As the sun rises, the High Chief stands at the Sacred Altar – it is a giant slab of stone – and makes a sacrifice. The sacrifice is most often a perfect white bull. The High Chief brings an ancient stone axe down to kill the bull, and then cuts the Beast's throat with a knife so its blood flows over the Altar. Most of our tools and weapons are made of stone, like that axe, or from animal bones. But I like best the copper ones that we get from traders. Their metal shines and glints in the sun, but the blades grow blunt so fast.

As ever, the mid-summer festival began when the crowd gathered together in the Great Temple as the sun set. There were too many people to count – young and old, families, friends, couples holding hands, everyone in

their best tunics. They ate and drank and drummed and sang and danced by the red flare of torch flames. Some had come from distant lands, but all are welcome at the Great Temple.

Two men stood at the side, watching. They were in the shadows, but I couldn't take my eyes off them. I wanted to work out where they had come from. They had swirling blue tattoos on their cheeks, their dark hair was in long braids, and each braid was tipped with a bead. Their tunics and kilts were made from deer-skin and they had leather bags slung over their bodies. They both carried bows, and quivers of arrows hung from their rawhide belts. They looked so alike, I was sure that they must be brothers. The older of the two had an ugly scar on his left knee, which I guessed would make him walk with a limp.

The night was short, and a faint glow in the east told us the sun would soon rise. The white bull was ready for the sacrifice. My father stood in front of the Sacred Altar and raised the stone axe. He wore the long black robe and ancient crown of antlers that every High Chief had worn before him. The white bull snorted, then lowered his huge head, almost as if he was telling my father that he was ready for the axe.

The bull's blood was our offering to the sun. It was the magic that the sun needed to stay alive as the nights grew long in the autumn. We would have to sacrifice another bull at the mid-winter festival, to stop the sun dying when the darkness of night was at its blackest and deepest. The crowd fell silent, everyone held their breath as they waited for the moment when the axe fell. The moment in which death and life would come together.

All of a sudden, the crowd shifted and moved and I heard angry voices call out. I looked round and saw Tigran shoving people out of the way as he and his warriors strode up to the Sacred Altar.

Tigran stood right in front of my father. I saw that he held another stone axe and its polished head shone in the light of the torches. His men bristled with weapons too, stone knives and spears with sharp flint blades in their hands and belts.

"What are you doing, Tigran?" my father said. "The moment is almost here ..."

"You are right, Daguno," Tigran said. "The moment is almost here – the moment of *your* death."

Then Tigran lifted his axe. He paused, with an odd look on his face. It was as if a battle was taking place in his mind. I looked over and saw that my father was looking at his brother with pity and love ... Then Tigran's face went hard and he smashed the axe down on my father's head. My father staggered back and fell onto the Sacred Altar and blood poured from his head onto the stone. I knew in my

heart that he was dead but even so I screamed out and ran over to him.

Tigran grabbed me. I struggled and tried to pull free, but he was too strong. He flung me down on the ground in front of the Sacred Altar. The bull bellowed and snorted. It was backing away, trying to get free, but nobody cared about that. People pushed forward, screaming with panic and fear. Tigran's warriors held them back, shoving at them with their spears.

"I have made the sacrifice!" Tigran yelled, and he glared at the crowd. "There is blood on the Sacred Altar! I will be your High Chief, and you will all obey me!"

"What about the boy, Maglos?" somebody called out. "He is his father's son and should be High Chief!"

Tigran turned and looked down at me. My blood ran cold.

"Maglos will soon be dead too," he said, as he lifted his axe again. "I will begin my rule as High Chief with another offering of blood for the sun. Daguno's son will give his blood too ..."

I closed my eyes and waited for the axe to fall.

Chapter 3
A Strange Pattern

I waited for the axe and for the darkness, but all I heard was more yells and screams. Then a powerful voice cut into the noise. I couldn't hear the words, but everyone fell silent. I opened my eyes and saw Tigran looking at someone. He pushed the crowd apart as he moved towards Tigran and me.

It was the man I had seen earlier, the one with the blue tattoos and braided hair. As he limped forward, people moved out of his way. His younger companion followed close behind. The man came up to the Sacred Altar and stopped in front of Tigran.

"You must not kill the boy," he said.

I heard that his accent was not like the people of our tribe. Where had he come from?

"Who are you to tell me what to do?" Tigran snarled. He slowly put down his axe and glared at him. I realised that I had been holding my breath till he did.

"Me? I am nobody," the man said with a shrug. "But the Gods will be angry if you stain the Altar with the blood of a child. It will bring a terrible curse down on your people. Look – even the sun waits to see what you will do. It should have risen by now ..."

The crowd turned to look at the faint glow of light in the east and gasped with fear. The sky was full of dark clouds and there was no sign yet of the sunrise.

"Tigran, what have you done?" someone shouted.

"Spare the boy!" another voice called out.

"Silence!" Tigran growled. I could see he was angry.

The crowd obeyed, but its mood was restless. Tigran looked down at me. I could see that again he was struggling to make up his mind. At last he did and then moved closer to the man. "I will let the boy live," he said. "But he must not stay here."

"Then perhaps I can help you," the man said. "I need a slave."

Up until then I had been lying on the ground, weeping in silence. I couldn't believe what had happened, and I was too frightened to make a sound or to move. But now I had a chance to live. And so I shouted out.

"I hate you, Tigran!" I screamed at him. "And I will make you pay for this!"

Then I jumped to my feet and flew at
him with punches and kicks. But Tigran just
laughed and held me at arm's length. He told
his men to tie me up, and they bound my wrists

with rawhide strips, so tight they bit into my skin and made it bleed.

"The boy is yours," Tigran said to the man, and then he shoved me at him as if I was a sheep or a goat that was no good to anyone. "He is yours – and good riddance."

At that very moment, the sun rose over the horizon. A gold ray of sun shot down onto the Sacred Altar and lit up the body of my father in a pool of his own blood.

The crowd roared, but I had to look away.

We left the Great Temple that morning. The man with the braided hair tied a rope to my wrists and pulled me behind him. The younger man kept looking over at me and tugged his brother's tunic as I stumbled along. But I didn't care about them, or about the people staring at us. I was lost in darkness. I hated my uncle and was sick with sadness for my dead father.

I didn't care where we went, but I soon saw we were heading south on the track that led to the forest. The two men stayed silent, and that was fine by me – I had nothing to say to them. The day grew hot, the sun shone in a blue sky. But I hated the sun now as much as I hated Tigran – it had shone its rays on my dead father. And that had felt like a betrayal – the sun could not be my friend.

At last we came to the forest. We walked into the cool shade under the trees, and the men stopped to make camp in an open space with oak, beech and ash trees all around it. The younger man collected dry leaves and twigs to make a fire and struck sparks from flints to get it started. His brother turned to me with a metal knife in his hand – and cut the rawhide strips away from my wrists.

"We are far from the temple now," he said. "You are free to go."

I stared at him, puzzled. "But … but I thought I was your slave."

"No," he said. "I would never keep a slave."

"I don't understand," I said. "Why did you save me if you don't want me as a slave?"

The man gave a shrug. "Because I could," he said. "It seemed better for you to live than to die. And better too for your people not to have a curse put on them."

"But what can I do now?" I said, and my eyes filled with tears. Everything I had ever known had been taken from me, and I was full of terror. "Where *can* I go?"

Just then the younger man appeared at his brother's side. He made signs with his hands and moved them in a strange pattern, as he pointed at me and nodded.

The older man turned to me and smiled. "My brother thinks you should stay with us, at least for now," he said. "But you can choose – you are free to go if you want to."

I stared at them for a moment. Then I felt the terror drain away. I was tired and I wanted to rest. I nodded. "Can I stay with you?" I asked.

But I was still lost in darkness, as I soon found out.

Chapter 4
Beautiful Things

The two men told me about themselves that evening. The older one was called Athir, and his brother's name was Caturix. They had come from a distant land, Athir said, far to the south, beyond the sea. Their country was a land of great mountains, so tall they almost filled the sky. Athir told me he had always been good at learning the languages of others, and had soon learned ours.

But Caturix couldn't say anything in any language. He understood what his brother said, and what I said too. But he could only talk with his hands, with those odd patterns that flowed from his fingers. Athir spoke back to him in the same way, with his hands.

"The Gods forgot to give my brother a voice when he was born," Athir said. "Yet he has made his own way of talking – and, with his hands, he talks more sense than most people."

The brothers smiled at each other, and I could sense the strong link between them. We were sitting round the camp-fire, and they had made a meal from the dried meat and nuts and berries they took from their bags. They enjoyed their food, and I tried to eat too, but the little I could eat sat like stones in my belly. When I saw how close they were, all I could think of was my father and how he was dead now, gone from me for ever. My grief was sharp.

Athir asked me lots of questions. But I gave him few answers, just my name, and a little of the story of what had happened at the Great Temple. At last, he stopped talking, and we

lay down to sleep under a dark, moonless sky. Caturix gave me a wolf skin to keep me warm, and I curled up on the hard ground, hugging myself, my mind full of pictures I could never forget. All night, I drifted in and out of sleep.

We left our camp early the next morning and headed south into the forest. The two brothers both carried bows – and they were skilled hunters, so we had rabbit to go with the dried nuts and berries for our meal that night. But still I didn't eat much, and I talked even less. Caturix tried hard. He smiled at me, offered me the best parts of the rabbit, and kept talking to me with his hands. But I ignored him.

That night, I curled up on the ground again, and I wished I was dead. Then, when the night was at its darkest, I had a sudden thought – my breath was moving in and out of my body, but perhaps I was dead already. My heart was a fire that had gone out and now there were only ashes. All I had to do was wait for the wind to blow those ashes away. Then my spirit would be free to travel to the Land of the Dead where my father waited for me ...

The next day we came to a village, and there I found out that Athir and Caturix were traders in metal. Their bags were full of beautiful things made from copper – knives, bracelets, a mirror so polished you could see your face in it. They also had necklaces of beads like the ones in their hair, but strung on copper wire instead. They laid everything out on a cloth on the ground, and an eager crowd gathered to trade.

After that, we moved on and set up camp in another part of the forest. And that's where I found out Athir and Caturix were not just traders in metal – they made it too.

I watched as they dug a small hole, filled it with twigs, then added two things they took from their bags – charcoal and some green stones. They set fire to the twigs, covered it all with soil, and blew air into the hole along a pipe made from a hollowed-out branch. The fire grew very hot – it became a deep red glow in the soil. When the fire faded, Caturix dug into the hole with an antler pick. He pulled out the stones, but they weren't green any more – they were partly black, but parts of them shone too.

Caturix knocked the black parts away with a flint, and soon he had a small pile of rough copper. He made another blaze, put the rough copper in a stone jug, and stood it in the hottest part of the fire. I saw how the copper melted and then Caturix put on thick gloves made of cow-hide so he could pick up the jug. Next he poured the liquid copper into a stone mould. It cooled in the mould until it was a solid, square lump of metal.

I was transfixed – the stones had turned into metal.

Athir looked up from the new lump of metal and smiled at me. "So now you know," he said. "If you find the right kind of stones, and heat them in the right way, you can turn them into copper. You need skill to work the metal and make it into a knife or a bracelet, but we can teach you how to do that, along with other secrets ... You can learn this craft, Maglos, if you want to. And I can see in your eyes that this magic – this secret of the stones – speaks to you."

He was right. For a brief moment something in this world – the Land of the Living – was important to me, and I had forgotten I was dead. But the darkness came back in a swift flood, and I could almost hear my father call to me from far away.

"There can be no more magic in this world for me," I said. "Nothing matters to me."

Athir opened his mouth to say something, but Caturix tugged his sleeve and spoke to him with his hands. Athir gave a sigh and nodded, then turned to me again.

"My brother thinks I should leave you alone, and I think he's right," he said. "But remember what I said, Maglos. When you are ready, we can talk about it again."

I nodded, but I didn't think I would ever be ready.

I was wrong.

Chapter 5
Shadow of the Past

We moved on, out of the forest and into a land of meadows and gentle rolling hills, passing from village to village. Summer changed to autumn, and then to winter, and the days grew shorter. On mid-winter night, the darkness inside me grew too deep to bear. I thought about my father, and about the Great Temple. I tried to push the thoughts from my mind, but it was just too hard.

A few days before, we had found a hut on a hillside, the kind that shepherds use when they take their flocks up into the hills for the summer. I lay in Caturix's old wolf skin beside the fire we had made, and sobbed. I didn't want Athir or Caturix to hear my tears. But it was no good – my crying was too loud.

Athir heard me. "This is the darkest night, Maglos," he said as he sat on the other side of the fire. "But the days will grow longer from now on. Remember how after mid-winter at the Great Temple, the days grow longer as the sun comes back again."

My tears stopped as I listened to him and fell into a deep and dreamless sleep. When I woke up, I felt refreshed. That moment marked a turning point. From then on the darkness in me faded as the days grew brighter. By the spring I felt almost like my old self again – it helped that the land was full of life and colour, the sky full of birds that chattered and sang and swooped. And it was then that I took up Athir's offer, and started to learn how to make metal.

I started to learn how to speak with my hands too, so that I could talk to Caturix – and I found out how he loved to tease.

"You're terrible at understanding me," he would say, as his fingers flashed to and fro. "And you'll never be as good as me at making copper. I'm right, aren't I, Athir?"

"Take no notice, Maglos," Athir said. "Caturix thinks he's the best at everything."

We talked like this many times as we worked or walked together. Athir became like a second father to me, and Caturix was the brother I'd never had. It was a joy to make copper, and I wished I had always done so. Athir and Caturix showed me how to craft things with the copper – how to melt the metal, how to carve wooden or stone moulds and how to pour the liquid metal into them.

The best part of all was when we broke the mould to find a beautiful object inside – a

bracelet or an arm-ring, a knife or a
spear-blade shaped like the leaf of a tree ...

Yet there were still times when the shadow
of the past fell over me like a storm cloud over
the sun. I thought of my father and my tribe
and the Great Temple. I thought how Tigran
would lead the rituals and make the sacrifices
instead of me. Anger would fill my heart, and
there were whole days when I would snap over
silly things. Athir and Caturix understood –
they were always gentle with me when I was
like that.

I sometimes day-dreamed about returning
to my village to defeat Tigran. I prayed to the
Gods to make that happen, but they didn't seem
to listen.

Then came the day when I knew the Gods
had heard me.

*

The next year we slowly made our way west. By the autumn we could go no further – we had come to the end of the land and there was nothing but sea beyond. There were only a few villages, but Athir said that didn't matter. He was looking for somewhere he had heard of, a special hidden place. We would find a different kind of stone there, he said, one that would help us make a new metal that was stronger than copper.

Athir knew the place as soon as he saw it, a cave under a rolling green hill. We crept inside the cave and dug out lots of grey stones with shiny white flecks. We filled our bags with them and over the next few days we worked on the stones. We melted them, and they produced little bits of white metal – which Athir called "tin". We then added that to the melted copper. Copper has a red tinge to it, almost like blood. But the new, mixed metal was a dark brown, the colour my skin turns when I have been in the summer sun.

Athir used the metal we created to make a small knife. He carved a handle from a thick deer antler, and polished the blade with a handful of fine white sand till it had a beautiful dull shine. Then he made the blade sharp. He ran a rough stone up and down the edge with a harsh raspy noise, doing it again and again until the tip felt sharp to his finger.

"This new metal is called bronze," he said, as he handed me the knife. "That's what your

people call it. I have heard other names in other lands – the tribes to the east and south of my home call it the Metal of the Gods. See how it is much harder than copper. It will keep its edge for a long time, and it will cut almost anything."

I held the knife. It was heavy in my hand as if it had some dark magic. *'Bronze,'* I thought, truly the metal of the Gods. Caturix gave me things to try it on – an old piece of leather, the rabbit bones from our meal, an arrow shaft. And it thrilled me to see that Athir was right – the blade sliced cleanly with no effort.

"Could we make another blade as sharp, but much bigger than this knife?" I asked.

"I have seen bigger blades made of bronze – they are called swords," said Athir. His eyes narrowed. "Why do you want such a thing?"

"Why do you ask?" I said as I met his gaze. "I want to kill Tigran."

42

Chapter 6
Fight to the Death

Athir and Caturix argued hard with me, but I would not listen. My mind was made up. Tigran must die. In the end, Caturix shook his head and gave up. But Athir had one final thing to say.

"You are too young to fight your uncle," he began. I opened my mouth to speak, but Athir held up his hand. "He is a man, a warrior, and you are a boy. I will help you to make a fine bronze sword, but you must be patient, you must give yourself time to grow and learn to be as skilled a warrior as him. Swear this to me now – or we shall be friends no more."

"My brother only wants to help you stay alive," Caturix said, with a flash of his fingers. "And you know what he is like – he always gets cross when he is troubled."

Athir glared at him, then turned back to me.

"How long will I have to wait?" I said. "It has been over a year since Tigran killed my father."

"Just as long as it takes, Maglos," Athir said, with that shrug I knew so well.

I sighed, and felt my whole body sag. "Very well," I said. "I agree."

Athir smiled. "Come, there is still light in the day for us to work by," he said. "I will ask the stones for secrets to make bronze fit for the sword of a warrior ..."

Three years passed before Athir thought I had grown enough and learned the skills I needed to fight Tigran. In those three years we travelled down many tracks, went to many villages and met many people. I was taller than both Athir and Caturix now, and strong too. I had learned as much as I could about how to make metal.

But Athir still knew more than Caturix and I put together.

There was some deep skill in Athir, in his sharp eyes and clever hands, something like magic. Caturix and I often made mistakes in our melting and making – our knives would turn out too soft or too brittle. Yet Athir always knew just what we had done wrong, and everything he made was perfect. To this day I have never seen anything as fine as the bronze sword he made for me.

It was fully as long as my arm. The blade was narrow from the hilt to half way down, then became broad towards the tip. Both edges were sharper than any knife. So sharp, in fact, that Athir made me a wooden scabbard covered in deer-skin so I wouldn't hurt myself when I hung the sword from my belt. Caturix made the sword handle out of the wood of an ash tree and carved a picture of the sun into it.

Athir and Caturix taught me their warrior dance, too. It was a good way to learn how to use the sword. I followed their steps, learned the pattern of the moves I would need in battle. The sword became part of me, as much a part of my body as my hands. I also learned what real fighting was like. We were attacked more than once on our travels, by those who wanted to steal from us or make us slaves.

It was after one of those fights that Athir said we could think about a return to my village. I had chased off our attackers on my own, but not before my sword had tasted their blood. Athir and Caturix stood and looked at me with smiles on their faces.

"If we leave soon, we should be at the Great Temple by mid-winter's night," Athir said.

I smiled back at them, and my heart beat in my chest like a drum.

We could hear the beat of drums in the Great Temple before we could see the giant stones. A stream of people flowed down the track to the Temple, the same as always – young and old, men and women, from near and far. The night was dark, and many people held torches, the red flames streamed in the cold wind, the harsh scent of smoke filled our noses.

I walked with Athir and Caturix and kept to the middle of the crowd. The three of us all wore wolf-skin cloaks with hoods to hide our faces. At last we came to the Great Temple and went in under the tall stones. We pushed deep into the crowd so we were close to the Sacred Altar.

Tigran stood there. He wore the black robe and antler crown that should be mine, and held the ancient stone axe. A perfect white bull stood beside him. The moment of life and death was near – and someone called out, "See! The sun comes!" The crowd all turned as one to look at the pale glow in the eastern sky, and everyone was silent.

Tigran raised the axe – and that's when I stepped forward. I threw off my cloak and drew my sword from its scabbard. The bronze blade shone in the torch light and dazzled Tigran. He looked at me, confused – then his eyes grew wide with shock. There were yells from the crowd, and some of Tigran's men moved towards me. But now Athir and Caturix threw off their cloaks and lifted their bows.

"Is it you, Maglos?" Tigran said, and his voice trembled. "I have seen you and my brother in my dreams many times – and begged you to forgive me for what I did."

He threw down the axe and sank to his knees in front of me.

"I have come to kill you," I hissed at him, and lifted my sword. He looked at me, then bent his head, ready for me to kill him. It made me think of the white bull that had lowered his heavy head on the night Tigran killed my father. I looked down at Tigran's head. It was so much like my father's. I thought of my father, and I knew he would not want me to do this.

I put my sword away.

"I will spare your life, Tigran, but I will not forgive you or let you stay here," I said. "Take off the robe and crown and go. I cast you out of this tribe for ever."

Tigran nodded. His eyes low, he did as I'd commanded, then fled. The crowd parted to let him pass. I put on the black robe and the crown of antlers and picked up the stone axe.

Then I stood for a moment to steady myself. I felt the crown heavy upon my head. It belonged to me now. Athir and Caturix stood behind me as the time came for the sacrifice.

I raised the ancient stone axe over the bull's massive neck just as the sun rose over the horizon.

The darkness was gone. Light filled my eyes and my heart.

I brought the axe down.

About *Secret of the Stones*

Stonehenge has fascinated people for thousands of years, from the time of the Romans right up to the present day. It's amazing to think that this great monument was built by people who didn't have cranes or bulldozers, just their own strength and cleverness, but it's true. Stonehenge must have taken enormous effort over a long time to build, so the people who built it must have had a very good reason to do so. Most historians think it was a temple, and it does seem to be linked to sunrise and sunset.

We don't know very much about what kind of people built Stonehenge. But we do know that others came from near and far to visit

Stonehenge and the ancient sites near by, like the stone circles at Avebury. Archaeologists have found lots of animal bones at these places, so there must have been great gatherings with music and feasting – a bit like our festivals today. Archaeologists have found tombs there too, so we know that important people were buried there.

In 2002 the body of a man was found during an archaeological dig close to the village of Amesbury, near Stonehenge. He had been buried with many things, including copper knives and a kind of small anvil. There were arrowheads in his grave too, so he was called the Amesbury Archer. Tests were done on his bones, and it was discovered that he was from the Swiss Alps, in Europe. It was even found that he had a knee injury which perhaps made him limp.

Some people think the Amesbury Archer might have been a travelling metal-worker.

He was alive in the time around 2300 BC, which was a period of change. For thousands of years, people had made tools and weapons out of stone and bone. Then came copper, which was better – but still not perfect. But then they discovered how to make bronze, and that was much better. In fact, people in mainland Europe worked out how to use bronze long before people did in Britain. To make bronze you add tin to copper, and tin could be found in the far west of Britain, in ancient Cornwall. There were tin mines in Cornwall for thousands of years.

All these aspects of history came together when I was thinking about the story that became *Secret of the Stones*. I found out that a second body had been discovered in Amesbury, a younger man related to the Archer. In my story, he became Caturix, a character who can't speak. I gave him his own special sign language – because I'd discovered that historians think such people in ancient times learned to communicate using their hands. After that the other characters fell into place – Maglos, Daguno, Tigran, as well as Athir and Caturix – so quickly that it felt as if they really had been alive thousands of years ago, and Maglos was simply telling me his story.

I hope you find it as fascinating as I did.